Flying

Lemurs

Zehra Hicks

TWO HOOTS

Lemurs are really good at jumping. Everyone in my family is brilliant at it.

Mum does a great trapeze jump!

Dad's masterpiece is
his trampoline jump.

Even Granny can jump!
Her cannon jump is superb.

It's my turn next.
It's going to be
the most amazing
jump **ever!**

One...

Two...

Three...

Uh-oh!

I can't do it.

Don't worry.
There are lots
of other jumps
you can do.

What about the
see-saw jump?

I'll do it with you!

Oh yes, I love the see-saw jump!
There's really nothing to it.

All I have to do is stand still
and wait for Granny.

One...

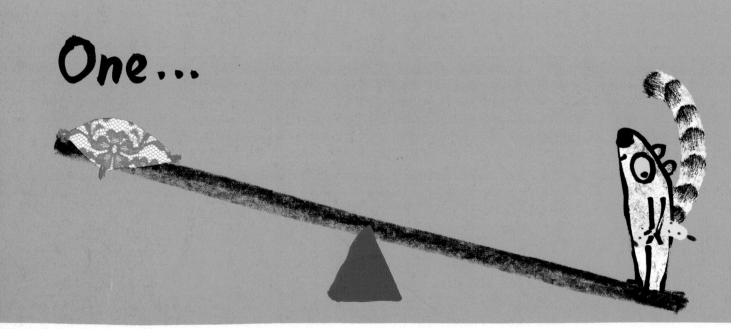

Two...

Come on Granny!

munch!
munch!

Three...

Here she
comes . . .

Uh-oh!

I can't do it.
(Sorry Granny.)

Don't worry. What about the hoops?
You're good at the hoops.

Oh yes, they're really easy.
Anyone can jump through a hoop!

One...

Two...

Three...

What a disaster!
I'm actually not good at jumping at all.
In fact, I'm really rather rubbish.

Don't worry. You don't have to jump.
There are lots of other things you're good at.

You're really good at having
the fluffiest ever tail ...

You're brilliant at playing
the tambourine ...

And you're fantastic at throwing custard pies.

Yes, I suppose I am quite good at having the fluffiest ever tail

playing the tambourine

and throwing custard pies.

In fact I'm quite good
at skateboarding too

and playing the
recorder upside down.

And I bet I can be a
really amazing rocket ...

Three...
Get ready.

Two...
Stretch up!

One...
Bend the
knees and . . .

Uh?

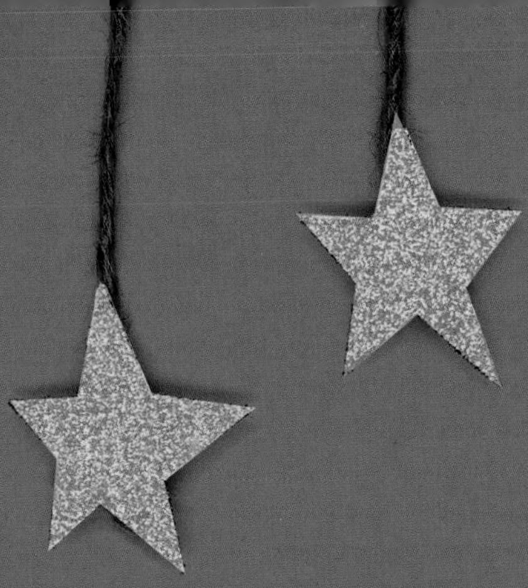

oooh!

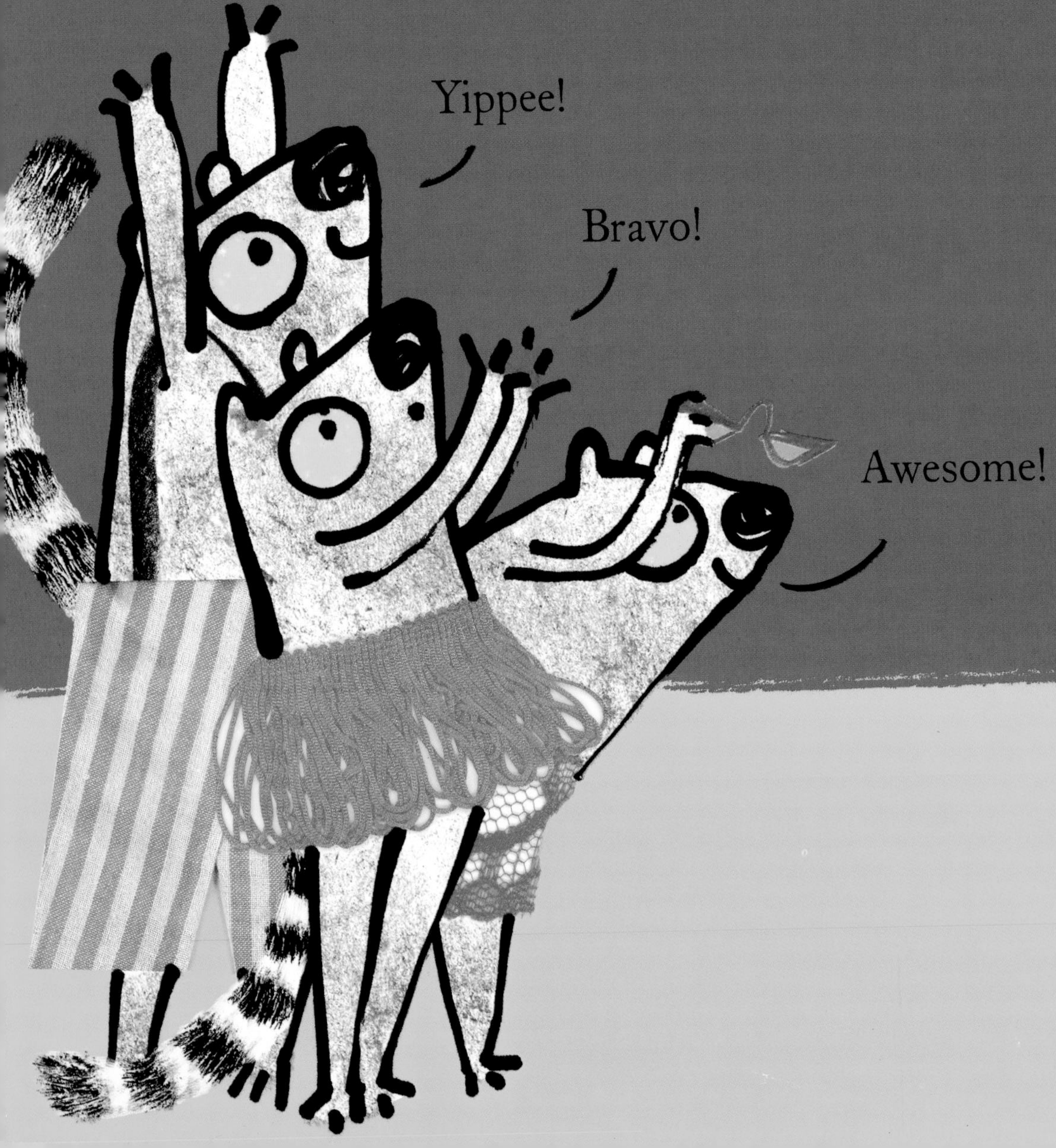

That's the most amazing jump
ever!